VIPER ATTACK

Cardiff Libraries
www.cardiff.gov.uk/libraries

Llyfrgelloedd Caerdydd
www.caerdydd.gov.uk/llyfrgelloedd

Bloomsbury Education
An imprint of Bloomsbury Publishing Plc

50 Bedford Square
London
WC1B 3DP
UK

1385 Broadway
New York
NY 10018
USA

www.bloomsbury.com

BLOOMSBURY and the Diana logo are trademarks of Bloomsbury Publishing Plc

First published in 2017 by Bloomsbury Education

ISBN: PB: 978-1-4729-2960-0
         ePub: 978-1-4729-2961-7
         ePDF: 978-1-4729-2962-4

2 4 6 8 10 9 7 5 3 1

Typeset by Integra Software Services Pvt. Ltd.
Printed and bound in China by Leo Paper Products

MIX
Paper from
responsible sources
FSC   FSC® C020056

This book is produced using paper that is made from wood grown in managed,
sustainable forests. It is natural, renewable and recyclable. The logging and manufacturing
processes conform to the environmental regulations of the country of origin.

To find out more about our authors and books visit www.bloomsbury.com.
Here you will find extracts, author interviews, details of forthcoming
events and the option to sign up for our newsletters.

recommended by

CatchUp®
www.catchup.org

Catchup is a charity which aims to address the problem of underachievement
that has its roots in literacy and numeracy difficulties.

MISSION ALERT
VIPER ATTACK

BENJAMIN HULME-CROSS

Illustrated by
Kanako and Yuzuru

BLOOMSBURY EDUCATION
AN IMPRINT OF BLOOMSBURY

LONDON OXFORD NEW YORK NEW DELHI SYDNEY

Tom and his twin sister Zilla go to a boarding school. They don't like it very much. But Tom and Zilla have a secret. They work as spies for the Secret Service. Sometimes there is a spy mission that children are better at than grown-ups. That's when Tom and Zilla get their next Mission Alert!

CONTENTS

Chapter 1

Tom was bored. He and Zilla were doing their Maths homework. Zilla liked Maths. Tom didn't. He was staring at fractions on the computer screen, wishing he could be outside playing football.

Suddenly his watch began buzzing.

On the watch screen were the words, "MISSION ALERT!" Tom jumped up with excitement.

"Zilla," he whispered. "It's our next mission! I wonder what we will have to do this time..."

Zilla looked at the same words on her own watch.

She and Tom plugged earphones into their watches. The watches had lots of special spy features. The Secret Service could find Zilla and Tom at any time by tracking their watches. They tapped the screens and the instructions began.

"Agents, here is your next mission," they heard Marcus say. Marcus was their handler at the Secret Service.

"We have an important guest in our country, and his son needs your protection while he is here. Please take a look at his file."

PROFILE: Charles Damba

From: Kenya

Age: 11

Height: 151 cm

Likes: rollercoasters, burgers, adventure stories and football

Security threat: no threat

"Charles's father is a scientist," said Marcus. "He has worked hard to sell medicines very cheaply in Africa. People who make medicines in Britain and the USA want to stop him so that they can make more money.

We have been tracking emails from a criminal gang called Viper. They are being paid to kidnap Charles Damba while he is in Britain."

"Why?" asked Tom.

"So they can frighten his father and force him to stop making cheap medicines!" said Zilla.

"That's right," said Marcus. "Tomorrow, Charles Damba will visit Wonder World Theme Park. We think that is where Viper will try to kidnap him. Your mission is to stop them.

There is just one problem. Charles's father has said that he does not want our help. So Charles won't know who you are. And he won't know that you are there to protect him."

Chapter 2

The next day, Tom and Zilla were outside the entrance to Wonder World Theme Park. They were at the front of the queue.

"This has to be the best mission ever!" said Tom. "Have you got the tickets yet?"

Zilla checked her watch. The Secret Service had said they would email her their entrance tickets.

"Yes, I've got them," said Zilla. "Just in time!" A woman was opening up the kiosk, to let people in to the park. Tom and Zilla showed her their tickets.

Just in front of them were three people dressed up in panda outfits. They were waving at everyone as they came into the park.

"That must be a really weird job!" said Tom.

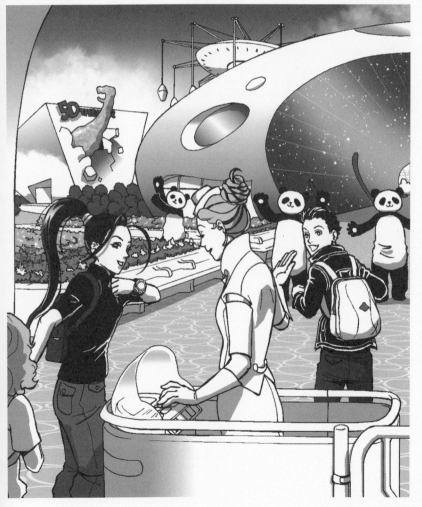

Tom and Zilla sat on a bench while they waited for Charles to arrive. They could see everyone who came into the park. Nobody looked like a kidnapper.

"Hey, there he is!" said Tom, pointing at a boy who had just finished paying for his ticket. He had two bodyguards with him. They were wearing black suits.

The pandas started making fun of the bodyguards, pointing at them and shaking their heads. The bodyguards ignored the pandas. Charles laughed and gave one of the pandas a high five before walking off towards the pirate ship ride.

"OK, you follow Charles and get talking to him if you can," said Zilla. "I'll stay here and see who comes in after him. Keep your watch on so I can get hold of you later!"

"Sounds good to me," said Tom. He ran off after Charles and his bodyguards. There was no sign of anyone who looked like a kidnapper. Tom watched as Charles went on the pirate ship ride. One of the bodyguards went with him. One bodyguard stayed at the entrance to the ride.

Tom pulled out a football from his bag. He hoped that Charles was as football-mad as Marcus had said. The pirate ship ride was coming to an end and Tom began kicking the ball hard against a low brick wall. After a few minutes, Charles came over to talk to him.

"Can I play?" he asked. He had a big smile on his face.

"No problem!" said Tom. This was perfect! Now he could stay really close to Charles without having to pretend he was doing something else.

"I'm Charles," said the boy.

"And I'm Tom. Nice to meet you!" said Tom.

A couple of the pandas walked past and sat down on a bench nearby. Tom and Charles had a bit of a kick around.

Then Charles wanted to go to the House of Horrors. Tom was excited. Wonder World had the biggest House of Horrors in the country.

The House of Horrors was on top of a large hill. On the way they could hear the shrieks from people on the White Water Washout ride. Halfway up the hill they saw a metal fence and some building machinery. A sign said:

MINERS' DOOM! NEW RIDE OPENING THIS SUMMER!

Chapter 3

Zilla had been waiting at the entrance for some time. She couldn't see anyone who looked like a kidnapper.

She was just about to go and look for Tom and Charles when something made her stop. One of the pandas suddenly walked away

from the crowds. It took off a furry glove, and pulled out a phone from its pocket.

Zilla got a bit closer to the panda and listened. She heard the panda saying:

"You two, stick to the plan. Just make sure he goes into the House of Horrors. If his new friend gets in the way, get rid of him! I will stay here and keep a look-out."

Zilla's heart was thumping. Then the panda dropped the phone. It skidded towards Zilla and she bent down to pick it up. So did the panda.

Their hands both touched the phone at the same moment, and that was when Zilla saw something that sent a shiver down her spine.

Whoever was inside the panda outfit had a green snake tattoo on the back of their hand!

The pandas must be the Vipers, thought Zilla. And they were going to kidnap Charles inside the House of Horrors! She had to warn Tom and Charles.

She jumped up quickly to rush away but she tripped over a bench and bashed her hand.

Zilla looked down at her watch screen, ready to call Tom. But she had smashed the glass screen of her watch when she fell.

Chapter 4

Charles's bodyguards were waiting for him outside the House of Horrors. Tom looked around. He was surprised to see two of the pandas in the queue behind him. Something didn't feel quite right.

"Lucky pandas!" said Charles. "They can go on the rides whenever they want!"

The pandas nodded their heads and waved at the boys to go on. If Tom had waited a few seconds longer he would have seen Zilla running up the hill towards them. But he turned away and went into the House of Horrors with Charles.

The boys made their way through the House of Horrors. Each room had a spooky surprise.

Then they walked into a room that was pitch black. The sound of clanking chains came from the speakers. They felt a gust of cold air on their faces. And then they both screamed as large hands clamped down on their shoulders.

Bright white lights began flashing on and off and they saw that the pandas were in the room with them.

At first, Tom thought they were playing around as they pushed and shoved him and Charles.

But as the shoving got rougher, Tom realised that something was really wrong. The pandas shoved the boys towards a large trapdoor in the floor.

Just then Zilla rushed into the room.

"They're not pandas," she shouted to Tom. "They are the Vipers!"

"They look more like pandas to me," said Charles.

Zilla ran at one of the Vipers but she just bounced off him. She crashed to the floor. Tom and Charles tripped over her and the Vipers shoved them all through the trapdoor.

Chapter 5

They landed in a pile on the ground. They could just see that they had landed in between two sets of narrow train rails.

There was an open-topped cart on each set of rails.

The first of the Vipers jumped down and landed next to them.

"It's only the Damba boy we want," he growled. "You two, get lost!"

"No way!" Tom shouted. "Come on!" He jumped into one of the carts. Charles and Zilla jumped in after him. The Viper tried to grab Charles but he missed as the cart began to roll along the rails.

The second Viper hit the ground next to the first. They began shouting at each other, then they jumped into the cart on the other set of rails and began rolling after Zilla and the boys.

"Who are you?" Charles shouted to Tom and Zilla.

"It doesn't matter who we are," Zilla yelled back. "But we are your friends and those pandas are not!"

They couldn't speak any more because the cart was rolling faster and faster down the track.

"This must be the Miners' Doom. The new ride that is opening in the summer," Tom shouted.

"They are just behind us," Zilla screamed. Charles and Tom looked back and saw the two Vipers on the other rails. They were catching up!

Tom tapped his watch screen and clicked
on the light beam app. A bright blue light cut
through the darkness. He shone it at each

of the Vipers' eyes in turn. They cried out and hid low down in their cart to get out of the way.

"I can see daylight. We are nearly at the bottom!" cried Charles. "Is this the brake?" He began pulling a lever. Then he yanked it hard. The three of them were thrown to the front of the cart.

The wheels jammed on the rails, sparks flew, and the cart came to a stop in the sunlight.

Zilla, Tom and Charles jumped out of the cart.

The Vipers' cart rushed out of the tunnel at full speed. They crashed through the fence at the end of their track and their wheels hit a low wall. The Vipers were thrown out of the cart. They flew through the air and landed with a huge splash at the bottom of the White Water Washout ride.

"Looks like they didn't find the brake!" said Charles.

The children heard Charles's bodyguards calling his name.

"We had better go!" said Tom. "It was fun meeting you!"

"Thanks for everything!" said Charles. "Can't you tell me who you are?"

"Sorry," said Tom. Then he and Zilla climbed over the metal fence and jumped down onto the path.

As they walked away, they saw the security guards pulling two men in very wet panda suits out of the water.

"Do you think we have time for an ice-cream now?" asked Tom.

Bonus Bits!

Quiz Time!

Check how well you paid attention to the story by answering these multiple choice questions. The answers are at the end of this section – no peeping!

1. What did Tom wish he was doing instead of Maths homework?

a playing football outside

b playing on his skateboard

c playing a computer game

d eating his dinner

2. What country is Charles Damba from?

a India

b Kenya

c South Africa

d Brazil

3. Why do some people who make medicines want to stop Charles's father's work?

a his work is bad for the environment

b they are worried he will hurt someone

c they don't like him

d they want to make more money

4. What is the name of the gang planning to kidnap Charles?

a Pandas

b Demons

c Vipers

d Spies

5. Why does Tom say "This has to be the best mission ever!"?

a because he gets to play a computer game

b because he gets to go to a theme park

c because he likes saving people from being kidnapped

d because he gets a free dinner

6. Which ride does Charles go on first?

a Pirate Ship ride

b Miners' Doom

c White Water Washout

d Haunted House

7. What did Zilla see that sent a shiver down her spine?

a a green snake in the bushes

b the panda chasing after a young child

c a smashed mobile phone on the floor

d a green snake tattoo on the back of the man's hand

8. Why could Zilla not use her watch to contact Tom?

a the man had taken it from her wrist

b the dial would not turn anymore

c the screen had smashed when she fell

d Jake did not have his turned on

9. What ride were the carts that the children and the pandas were in?

a Pirate Ship ride

b Miners' Doom

c White Water Washout

d Haunted House

10. Why did the pandas end up in the water on the White Water Washout ride?

a they didn't use the brake on the cart

b the police were chasing them

c the children knocked them off the tracks

d the bodyguards were chasing them

What are Vipers?

Vipers are venomous snakes found in many parts of the world. They have long, hinged fangs that allow them to bite into their prey and inject venom. When they are attacking, they can open their mouth to nearly 180 degrees.

So, pretty scary creatures! No wonder the mean criminal gang in this story called themselves 'The Vipers'!

What Next?

Have a think about these questions after reading this story:

- Why do you think Charles's father did not want the Secret Service to help? What might he think would happen?
- How do you think Charles would have felt if the children had not been there to save him?

ANSWERS to QUIZ TIME!
1a, 2b, 3d, 4c, 5b, 6a, 7d, 8c, 9b, 10a

Look out for Tom and Zilla's next spy
mission, ISLAND X.

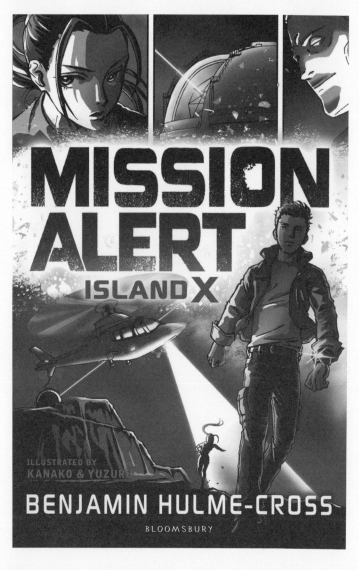

ISBN 978-1-4729-2956-3

Here is a sneak preview!

Chapter Five

Simpson led Tom and Zilla down to the huge machine. Boris Silver was standing there. He had a nasty smile on his face.

"I **knew** you were here to cause trouble!" said Boris Silver. "Of course, I won't be able to let you go now. You've seen too much."

"Did you really think there weren't any guards on duty tonight? I knew you wanted to see inside these secret buildings and I wanted to catch you in the act!" Silver laughed.